Behind the
Boarding School

Rebecca Victoria Winnard

PUBLISH AMERICA

PublishAmerica
Baltimore

First printing

ISBN: 1-4137-6777-X
PUBLISHED BY PUBLISHAMERICA, LLLP
www.publishamerica.com
Baltimore

Printed in the United States of America

For Mummy, who has taught me much
and loved me even more.
Thanks for everything.
I love you to bits!

Contents Page

Introduction

Boarding school offers a unique education in many ways. It is the sort of social and character-forming education that lasts a lifetime. Every school has its own particular traditions but there are similar threads that run through every school. These similarities fall into three main categories: social skills, expectations and the development of the "all rounder" personality.

Particular social skills (described in "Boarding School Manners and Social Norms") and a respect for others are an important philosophy. There is a strict discipline most notably in the younger years but as the pupils reach the sixth form they are treated as adults and are allowed more of a free reign. The sixth form are granted more responsibility in organising the younger years e.g. they are solely responsible for organising inter-house events.

Everyone is encouraged to stand out and there is an unwritten rule that it is a great accomplishment when the Head knows your name! There are academic prizes awarded at the end of the year but also sports scarves are given to those who play in the first XI teams. It seems to be a common misconception that people at boarding school are consistently talking about the amount of money they have, but in reality, people are respected for having confidence, popularity or generally being good at something whilst the family they are born into is not important.

The philosophy to capitalise on the talents that you have, or indeed, to develop new ones, is the basis for the encouragement of the confident all-rounder. Drama, public speaking, sports and voice lessons are part of the curriculum. Private lessons for instruments and drama are offered at an extra cost.

There are regular events in the school where pupils can perform in both music and drama. This is good practice for performing in front of an audience! Sports matches are held throughout the year against other schools and there are also popular inter-house matches. If you want an alternative to sport, art and drama, people are encouraged to contribute their time to local charities or think of new ways of raising money. The vital point is that the pupils leave with the self-belief that they can do anything. It is this confidence that leads to being successful in many areas of life. Another important skill is the ability to balance many activities effectively hence having a good work/life balance in the future.

The academic year is separated into three terms. At the third weekend of each term, there is an exeat weekend where everybody goes home, or if they live abroad, then people stay with friends.

Each person is attached to a boarding house where they sleep and relax. The houses have recs that are full of unmatching comfy chairs, the all important television and other games. There are kitchens to make simple food and house the toaster that feeds the average boarder's fixation with toast.

In case of any illness there is another house called san that is staffed by nurses twenty-four hours a day and the school doctor visits twice a week.

In order to get into the senior school, it is necessary to pass the entrance exam and an interview. Most schools have particular feeder prep schools from which a large percentage of their annual intake is chosen. In this book the people who went to the prep school are referred to as preps.

The best way to explain what boarding is like is through the eyes of a new pupil who is starting at a girls' boarding school at age eleven. She will show you a typical year exactly the way she sees it, without exaggeration or editing, and you can make up your own mind, but it is actually a *really good laugh*!

Boarding School Manners
and Social Norms

Question: Admittedly, this is an incredibly complex area, but what sort of behaviour can you expect from boarding school kids?

Answer: The technical etiquette such as giving up your chair for elders, knowing which knife and fork to eat with etc is easily learnt but the main emphasis that underlies all manners is the idea that potential embarrassment or awkwardness should be minimised as much as possible. This helps all social interaction run as smoothly as possible so, although flexible, the following points are guidelines that help to achieve this aim.

Top tip: never ignore people. In fact, pick up on what they say and elaborate on it. The only thing that should be ignored is that you might not know everyone in the group but talk to them as though you have always known them - that way strangers become potential friends!

When somebody joins a group mid-conversation, they should be given a quick summary of the conversation so that it makes it easier for them to join in.

Avoid tense subjects that could lead to a passionate argument by glossing over it as humorously as possible. (Naturally, not applicable to debating or English lessons!)

Always keep situations humorous even when talking about potentially sticky ideas. In a typically English fashion, this is helped by using understatement to appear calm and less offensive.

Teasing is a form of friendliness because it is based on the assumption that nobody is going to be rude therefore it is a joke. It is a way of saying, "Great, we don't have to be formally polite with you now because you are one of us."

Put a positive slant on people when talking about them - I have lost count of the number of times I have heard the phrase, "I am sure they are lovely/ really nice." It is also normal to relay a story about a situation without adding any obvious value judgements, e.g. "horrid, arrogant creep," but leave it to the story and the phrasing to do the work for you.

Support each other when people succeed at things - success is good!

Help out in a dilemma when you can and the favour is always returned.

Discretion.

This deserves a section to itself simply because it is so important. It is vital to know when to say things and to whom; if in doubt, don't! It is always best to cover up for people and not repeat their drunken antics to their parents.

Don't show shock in any situation. This is useful for when your pinstriped-trouser-suited business partner admits to a passion for dressing in drag with a spot of pole dancing and running an underground drug network in his spare time. It is very useful to adopt the diplomatic blank expression and treat it as though it is the most normal thing in the world. There is beauty in diversity!

Brush any resolved problems and arguments away and carry on as though nothing has happened.

Don't dob each other in, i.e. don't get people into trouble for smoking or anything else that they are not meant to do. If a member of staff asks if you know anything about an incident, deny all knowledge - people have to stick together.

Now that your head is spinning, let's get to the story and put some of the rules into context...

Annual Events

Autumn Term

Welcome Tea
Inter-house Lax and Hockey Matches
1st - 3rd Year Social
6th Form Ball
Music and Drama Exams
Dorm Decs
Head's Party
Christmas Church Service

Spring Term

Snowball Fights
Drama Productions
School Birthday (Celebrate with junk food lunch then sing Happy Birthday to the school, and after that, the whole dining hall will stamp their feet whilst remaining seated)

Summer Term

Inter-House Fashion Show
Strawberry Tea
6th Form Trip to Wimbledon
Social
6th Form Ball
Sports Day
Mini Speech Day
Leavers' Weekend

Autumn Term

Dear (*insert your name here*),

Well played for passing the entrance exam and choosing this school. Everyone knows that boarding might be a bit different if it is away from all of your previous friends but do not worry because everyone has gone through this before and survived to actually quite like the place. Let me introduce myself, I am your house ma and will be the person to show you around house and talk to if you get homesick or have any other dilemmas such as not being able to find the kitchen.

I shall meet you in the Great Hall when you arrive for the afternoon tea (the food is always nice at those things, so eat up or you will be left to munch on toast up at house all evening) and shall just be around for you to ask me any questions about school life so do not be afraid to ask away.

All that is left to say is that I hope you enjoy the rest of the summer and I look forward to seeing you in September at the Welcome Tea.

See you around.
House Ma X

The postcard had arrived during the summer holidays before the autumn term began and is, so far, the only introduction to my "house ma." Each year, the fifth form (who are the eldest in the house) adopts a first year who are known as "house kids" and look after them up at house. From what I understand, a house ma is the person who gets summoned by the rest of the dorm if the house kid becomes homesick or they simply pop in for a chat every so often.

The house mas are in the same boarding house as the first years but are given a little more prestige because they no longer share a dorm with eight people and now have the luxury of their own room complete with study desk and washbasin. It is only a year before the fifth form move up to the sixth form boarding house in a separate part of school but the house kids would have settled in by then and know the routine.

A letter from school has arrived detailing all of the uniform requirements and the added information that I will be joining St. Andrew's house. It is because of this that they have instructed very particular styles of nametapes to be added to every item of uniform and sports kit that needs to be washed in the school laundry. St. Andrew's house colour is blue so the nametapes have to be in blue letters on a white background plus the capital letter A after the person's name. The amount of uniform bought has to be double what is normally expected because the laundry is only returned weekly, so whilst one set of uniform is washed, there has to be a spare set to wear for that week.

The uniform is an important reflection of the school ethos so it deserves a detailed description. The skirts are grey A-line and strictly two inches below the knee. Any form of make-up is forbidden as is jewellery with the exception of a gold necklace and cross and/or signet ring. The only allowances for body piercings are one pair of gold "sleeper" earrings in the lower part of the ear and anything else will have to be removed during school hours.

(*This is to indicate from a young age that the emphasis is not on dressing scantily to attract men but on developing individual abilities and talents. There is no pressure to look either attractive or "grown-up" on a daily basis, just smart rather than doll- like. At this important stage of development, the focus is repeatedly upon building self-esteem based on what each person is capable of achieving.*)

Long-sleeved blouses are composed of narrow stripes, alternating between pale grey and white that are *always* to be tucked into the skirt. (*Yes, the word "always" really has to be noted because there is a great emphasis laid upon a smart appearance, so watch out if you dare to contravene school uniform rules.*) The woolly socks match the dark grey of the skirt and are pulled up to the knee. Shoes are also regulated with two simple styles of black leather lace ups without a heel only to be allowed in school. Judging by the amount of steps I remember I am quite glad about that otherwise I shall be in danger of breaking my neck. Ouch.

For the winter weather there is, of course, a jumper. It is burgundy and shows the classic v-line neck so that the collar of the v-line of the blouse can fit over the top of it. To finish the look, there is a burgundy blazer with fitted shoulder pads (alas, just looks stiff on first years), two buttons down the front of the blazer and the school crest sown on in gold cotton to the breast pocket. Beneath the school crest is the school dictum: *"Deo Soli Sit Honour Et Gloria."*

When it is very cold, there is a thick, ankle-length, grey (as you must be beginning to expect) woollen cloak lined in burgundy. It has two rectangular slits for arms to fit through but to complete the look there is a large hood that falls over the front of the top of the face making it quite difficult to see where to walk.

This is only the beginning. Uniform two is the "Formal Uniform" for special events in the school calendar, church on Sundays and any time when leaving the school grounds and representing the school, such as visits to the orthodontist. The socks, blazer and the style of the skirt are the same as the ordinary uniform but the skirt is black and slightly itchier. The burgundy and white striped blouses are long sleeved with cuffs and a collar up to the neck finished off by a one-centimetre wide burgundy piece of silk that has to be tied into a tight bow roughly seven centimetres wide and leaving ten centimetres hanging down. Phew, have you got that?

The list continues with a sports kit consisting of: burgundy knee-length socks, knee-length grey skirt that is pleated around the back but has a straight wrap around at the front. The blouse is a simple white aertex that has the wearer's initials sown onto the collar. Hockey/lax boots, hockey stick, lax stick, tennis racket, black fleece jogging bottoms, burgundy bags, trainers and indoor shoes finally complete the list.

Don't forget that there are beloved home clothes to wear outside of school hours, towels, posters, pins and other "must have" stuff that a room collects that might look surplus to others but a room would be characterless without them.

There are soooo many things that it is amazing they all fit into the trunk! But fit they must, and after some careful sit-downs on the trunk lid and squash moments, all is bolted up and ready to go. So, with the required "Formal Uniform" on, it is the time for delighted parents to take some pictures for the family album before leaving for the Welcome Tea.

The car speeds on through relentless windy roads and past fields until it approaches a small town that appears to be placed in the centre of eternal greenery. The journey gives time to meditate on what the evening will bring and what everyone will be like. Some friends from my prep school will be there as we all move up to the senior school together which is lovely even though we have not much idea of what to expect. Quite exciting really. The only introduction that we have had to the school life is on Friday morning when all of our year joined the main school for assembly in the Great Hall.

Looking out of the car window shows that the houses are well spaced, quaint and made out of traditional slate and stone that had been mined here previously. Large trees and mountains covered in heather produce a picturesque backdrop to the scene. The employment has turned towards the shops in the town of which there are relatively few, still, there are some chocolate shops so it should be ok. It is changing to dusk and the shops have all closed leaving the town to become peacefully empty with the exception of the town's pub and obligatory Chinese takeaway.

At last, turning sharply through a side street, the road widens to produce a tall gate painted in black with gold tops, and whilst normally they are closed, tonight they are wide open. The gates that represent a barrier between what is known and what is feared through being unknown is temporarily brought down; we are going behind the gates of boarding school.

The Arrival

Quite fortunately, the gates are stretched open because, for all of the people arriving in school for the term, there is only one entrance and exit, resulting in absolute chaos. The buzz of the sleepy town seems to be fixed upon this spot that has become the lifeblood of the area. The driveway is roughly wide enough for one and a half cars to pass because it is a throwback to when the school was built and people travelled by horse and cart, thereby requiring considerably less road space.

The solution is to do what the British do best and wait in a queue whilst all of the large cars edge towards the double gate. It is an opportunity for parents who have become good friends to simply put down the car windows and lean over for an amicable chat since nobody is currently moving anywhere.

Once through the gate, the narrow lane opens up to reveal the main school that had been hidden from view. To the left there is a large manicured lawn in front of the main school building with vividly coloured flowers in the borders.

The road snakes around the corner to the right to reveal the central part of the school and the main quad. The lawn of the quad is immaculate due to the fact that nobody is allowed to walk on the grass but the rule is certainly effective in maintaining the beauty of the place. Buildings surround the three sides of the quadrangle that are not occupied by the single road and these form the crux of school life in the centre of the campus. The view from the road is that on the right-hand side is the dining hall; to the left is the Great hall and a long corridor bridges both to form a large U shape.

The striking architecture is true to the nature of the time that the school was built when the windows were large arches with leaded lines running through them set amongst a natural grey stone wall. Although the predominant feature is grey, it is not severe due to the many intercepting features and the natural grass of the quad.

In the epicentre of the corridor, there is the main entrance with four stone steps leading to a double door made in oak, several metres above this the wall finishes in a bell tower (no idea what that is for yet).

As these musings continue, the car is parked around the side of the main building and it is time to progress to the Great Hall where, my introductory letter instructs me, the Welcome Tea will take place. At this point, I spot some other freshly pressed Formal Uniforms walking around and recognise it to be a couple of my friends from the preps. Hurrah! We greet each other with a friendly hug and continue to the Great Hall with parents in tow.

It is so lovely to see everyone again at this great opportunity to chat about the holidays and anything else that they have picked up about the life in house. Somebody has heard about a "Christening In" ceremony but they have been instructed by the older girls that under no circumstances are they to ask a member of staff about it. "What is it for?" or "What happens?"

It transpires that the ceremony happens in each boarding house and every first year has to undergo a trial that is decided upon by the "Dorm Head." Upon completion of this, the first year can then proudly consider themselves a full lifetime member of their house. Any person who joins later on in school life is exempt due to respect for their seniority. It sounds like an undercover conspiracy, so of course everybody keeps quiet, partially because it is exciting and it is also unthinkable to dob anybody in.

Many whispers abound about people having their heads flushed down the loo or even (gasp) being dangled from windows (please let that be an exaggeration!). Can it really be true that first years are made to run through the centre of the dorm whilst being completely naked? We shall just have to wait and see, but if it is just too much, then, thankfully, nobody can force you into doing anything.

Entrance to the Great Hall through a side door is the first sight of the interior today. The view from this end means that you can see everything. On the opposite end of the incredibly long and tall hall is a theatre stage raised roughly two metres from the ground and goes seven metres back behind velvet stage curtains that have been fully drawn (probably to hide the mess of various props from the parents).

Above the stage and sitting comfortably below the ceiling is a subtly coloured moulding of the school crest and school dictum. The floor is made of polished wood, which, coupled with the white walls and tall windows, provide a feeling of space. It is here that long tables covered in a white cloth have been temporarily laid out with metal platters of triangular-cut sandwiches (ham, beef, salad, egg or cheese) in both white and brown bread, placed next to shortbread, chocolate cakes, flapjacks and small sponge cakes. China plates and paper napkins are placed at one end of the table where everyone begins to queue.

The "Christening In" is forgotten because other activities begin to take away the main attention as most of the ex-preps, obviously used to school food made en mass, are preparing for tomorrow by piling the plates high with the chocolate cakes and biscuits that have been laid out for us.

The point of this tea is to meet the tutors and find out which of the two tutor groups we are going to be in. The tutor is a teacher in school who we register with twice a day to make sure that we are not avoiding any lessons, and also, they are somebody who we can talk to about any problems in school should any occur.

Well, we are left in suspense no longer. Tutor number one, Mrs Grey-Lloyd, sweeps into the room, delights in a suspensory pause to make sure that she has the small, surrounding group's attention, holds her arms up to just below her shoulders with palms facing outwards and introduces herself with perfect diction.

"Hello, girls, how is everyone?"

Yes, do not be left in any doubt, the whole world is her stage, for this is a fantastic representative for the drama department that she heads. Her hair is in short, flambuoyant silver curls that bounce as she walks. Today's clothes are: long camel boots that concertina at the top, knee-length cashmere skirt in the corresponding colour and a top hidden by a sweeping shawl that has been flicked around her body from the neck to the waist. The conversation turns to our experience of drama and had we made any new friends yet, to which we all answered politely and enthusiastically.

Amongst the growing crowd of pupils and parents is the second tutor: Mr Coward. Despite his name, this man does not have the stature of a victim but is tall and broad with a large smile and welcoming manner. He is Head of Music, so no doubt we shall see more of him later.

Silence is called for and a deadly hush rapidly descends upon everyone as a welcome "Sure, you will like it here" speech is read out by the tutors. After this, the first years are split into two groups, which had been decided previously, and this is to be our tutor group for five years.

With the greetings now over, our house mas have entered the hall to find us and take us up to house. This process is done with slightly less organisation than previous events but nonetheless effectively. The house mas approach each group and ask for a particular person's name before beginning a mutual introduction. Bless them; they try not to terrify the first years by being as approachable as possible, even though they do look terribly adult and assured to someone who is just eleven years old.

First Night

The three main boarding houses are opposite the Great Hall set back upon the top of thirty steps in the shape of a semi-amphitheatre (amphi). They are imposing buildings made of grey stone but softened with wallflowers and large balconies stretching across half the length of each dorm. There are narrow metal ladders built into the exterior wall to act as fire escapes from each dorm. The feel of space is created by the use of large leaded windows on the ground floor with smaller arched windows lining the walls of each dorm. The three main houses are grouped together, but St. Andrew's is set slightly further back than the other two and is at the top of another thirty steps in the centre of the amphi.

The hike to St. Andrew's is now over, and once my parents can bring themselves to leave me, usually with a big hug (ahhhh), it is in the capable hands of the other boarders to help everyone settle in. The house mistresses have emerged from their duty room (staff room) on the ground floor to greet everybody and to allocate them a dorm. There are four main dorms with fifth form rooms branching off the corridors. On the first floor the dorms begin with the prefix "Bottom" and the second floor called "Top," followed by right or left as appropriate.

"*Brace yourself,*" (said under my breath) problem number one: THE TRUNK. Thankfully, the porters have carried the tardis thus far, but now I'm on my own, as the porters are busy with the next load of luggage. The trunks are stored in the back of the house in a dark room (drag) with white-washed stone walls and a ceiling so low that even I, a first year, have to stoop down slightly.

The smell is dank and horrid due to no windows and pipes that run openly along the walls. In the centre of the drag is one single light bulb, so all in all, it is not really a meeting place. Yes, I do remember thinking about "needing" everything, but it is going to be a dilemma trying to get things from the ground floor up to the dorm two flights up.

This time there are no porters to carry the arm-stretching box, oh no, the inner contents are enough. There is a definite plus to this arrangement; after an uncountable number of trips up the stairs, I am unlikely to get lost in the future. It is soon easy to spot the more experienced border who will run to the cupboards to claim one of the scarce blankets to tip all of the contents of the trunk into.

Stage two is to find some willing friends who will haul the heaving blanket up the stairs with you but don't forget that the idea of eight people pulling the blanket at the same time might sound appealing but the favour has to be returned. It is seems to be fairly easy to find people to do this because all that really needs to be done is to approach someone who is sliding down a banister or is otherwise unoccupied.

Time for a little note of etiquette:
Nobody will bother to appear surprised or aggressive because it simply is not done. The etiquette is always to ignore that somebody is a stranger as much as possible and to converse easily with him or her. The only time to note that you do not actually know somebody is when they are initially introduced to you. The rules have evolved that way over time to facilitate the introduction and acceptance of people into a group with minimal awkwardness.

None of this occurs in isolation, on the contrary, friend-finding leads to a background of jubilation and excited exchange of gossip as friends who live on either side of the globe are reunited.

Surveying the dorm provides a fantastic reason for procrastinating the task of unpacking, so let's have a look. The dorms are made for eight people with a sample of two people from each year (1st - 4th). The layout of the dorm reflects the hierarchy of each age group, and inevitably, lowly first years are at the bottom by the door. There is a metre-wide aisle that runs down the centre of the dorm and splits it into two identical sections.

The living space (cubi) of each person is shared with someone else in their year. The cubi is roughly three metres squared and contains: a plain wooden packti, a sink, two single built in beds, a mirror and grey pin boards. It is customary that in each dorm the first and second years are in the front half of the room and the third and fourth years are in the back half. A low curtain rail separates the junior from the senior areas to protect privacy without blocking communication.

Outside every dorm is a short corridor ending in a fire door. In this space is: a shared bathroom, a separate toilet and a laundry cupboard. All of the amenities are plain white without any decoration surplus to requirements and the walls are painted a neutral white.

As the consuming process of unpacking begins, the dorm head (fourth year by default) will introduce themselves and will want to talk to "their" first years, usually out of a combination of curiosity and a motherly concern to see who will be in their dorm for the next fourteen weeks. The Dorm Head doesn't appear to have much authority apart from the official duty of sorting out midnight feasts at the end of term, but since there was too much else to talk about, I have no more detail to relay about that just yet.

The dorm head first of all congratulates me on choosing St. Andrew's house because it is most definitely the *best* house. It seems that I have inherited a house with a reputation of being daring and "naughty" so it sounds great to me. Andyites (pupils in St. Andrew's) are also known for being good sports for participating in any inter-house competitions and sports day, even though they might not always win (but it is not worth offending anyone by saying the last bit, gasp).

The other main houses are St. George's and St. Patrick's (Pats). Georges is the well-behaved house and always tend to win things (huge rival to Andies) whilst Pats has the enviable reputation of being incredibly friendly and hosting good parties. Each house thinks that they are the best house, but we in Andies know that we have the edge.

Friendly inter-house rivalry is encouraged and built upon to create a sense of pride in "belonging" to a particular house that never actually leaves the individual. The main purpose is to engender teamwork and a team spirit where people do their best in all areas of life so that they are not letting their house down which would be a great shame on the individual. Competitive inter-house sports matches and other events such as fashion shows foster this teamwork attitude. All of the age groups take part but are usually supervised by the sixth form who are given the responsibility of organising everything from the teams to the fashion show choreography.

As pupils progress through the school, they are given responsibility for their age group and below. It helps to build confidence without pupils realising that they are learning not only management skills for later life but are looking after the younger years.

And so the chatter continues way past lights out, that's 9.30 p.m. for first and second years, and who knows what tomorrow will bring?

Daily Timetable

7:20 a.m. First bell
7:30 a.m. Second bell and lights on
7:40 a.m. Third bell and should really start to move
7:58 a.m. Open side door of dining hall to let in late sixth form
8:00 a.m. Breakfast
8:30 a.m. Register with tutor
8:40 a.m. Assembly
9:00-10:15 a.m. Lessons followed by twenty minute break
10:35-1:00 p.m. Lessons
1:00-2:10 p.m. Lunch
2:10 p.m. Register with tutor
2:15-4:00 p.m. Lessons
4:45 p.m. Prep
5:30 p.m. Tea
6:00 p.m. Prep
6:45 p.m. Free Time
9:00 p.m. Lights Out for First Years (officially)

Breakfast

The first bell rang at 7:30 a.m. Not a soul stirred. Over a minute later the door was pushed open and the dorm lights were pressed on to reveal their brilliance. The only movement is the synchronisation of eight people turning over to block out the light and the associated imminent process of getting up. The house mistress swiftly makes her way around each person in the dorm to wake them up and occasionally rings the bell near the ears of the known offenders whom only run out of house in time for breakfast. Ten minutes later, another bell rings, and as this seems to suggest that getting dressed is now becoming urgent, I get out of bed, as do a couple of others. It's freezing. Time for a quick wash and to put on the well-ironed uniform.

At ten to eight, the house mistress gathers the first years together and shepherds them downstairs, through the amphi, across the quad (no, not on the grass, that is just sacred stuff) and through the wooden corridors of school to reach the double doors that herald the entrance to the dining hall. In the hall there is a buzz of activity because people from other houses all dash here for breakfast at 8:00.

The hall is roughly one hundred metres long and just incredibly high with the same arched windows that are seen in the rest of school. There are several long banqueting tables able to seat twenty people laid out in vertical lines parallel to the length of the hall. The tables are made of solid oak, as are the high-backed chairs that are neatly pushed away underneath the tables. Tables are on each side of the hall but there is a gap between the two sections down the length of the room.

Directly opposite the double doors at the end of the hall is the horizontal table called "High." This sacred table is raised on a small platform, and at breakfast, it is reserved exclusively for members of staff (*just to emphasise their authority, hence, increasing the respect from the pupils*). Traditionally, the head mistress will sit on a chair aligned in the centre of the other chairs looking outwards so that she can survey the entire room. The head's chair is a carver version of the plain oak chairs and has the school badge modelled onto the top of the chair with small rams carved next to it.

To the left of the tables is the canteen where there is a choice of cereal for people to help themselves to but can only take the bowls back to the tables and are not allowed to begin eating just yet. As the time ticks closer to 8:00, people move more frantically and sit in their allotted house tables. All of the years are mixed, but each boarding house has a particular block of tables reserved for members of that house.

Suddenly, the Prime Warden walks up to "High" and rings the hand bell that is in front of head's chair and says a rather cryptic phrase: "Can third years do chairs after breakfast." This is a statement rather than the suspected question, so they obviously do not have a choice in the matter, whatever that matter might be. Everyone stands behind their chair in silence, followed quickly by bewildered first years, bar the ex-preps who have always eaten here and know exactly what to expect. What on earth is going on?

The double doors open and in walk all of the house staff two by two in disciplined silence. They walk through the aisle between the two halves of the dining hall and take their places on "High" with the most senior member taking Head's Chair. Next, head's bow down and the following prayer is said by the person at Head's Chair: "For what we are about to receive, may the Lord make us truly thankful." The entire room joins in for "Amen," followed by a loud noise as hundreds of chairs are pulled back for people to then sit down.

On each table are two plain metallic milk jugs that are passed from the sixth form downwards in descending year order so first years go a little hungry for a bit longer than the others. Everyone chats to each other for a bit regardless of age or if they know them which makes it a really effective to get to know other members of the house.

There are rumblings around the table about sending a first year off to get "stuff." I am shown the way back to the canteen by a second year called Sarah where we enter a queue of seven people who are all waiting for "stuff." This turns out to be several small bread rolls in a variety of: wholemeal, white with poppy seeds and plaits of brown bread served upon a silver platter. It is dutifully taken back to the table and given to the upper sixth for first pick (first time I have ever wanted to be older because only the plain brown rolls are left for us).

To prepare for the scramble for butter, jam, chocolate spread, etc. the trick is to take a clean knife, dig into the spread and leave it on your side plate (everyone has their own side plate to their left) before stuff is called for.

Breakfast lasts for approximately twenty to twenty-five minutes and is ended when the staff on "High" stands up and leaves, at which point people are free to follow and go to their tutor groups.

P.S. If you linger a little longer, the mystery of "doing chairs after breakfast" is revealed as clearing the plates off the tables, taking large stacks of them to the kitchen and pulling the chairs from under the tables so that the kitchen staff can clean under the tables much more easily. It looks like a gross job because all of the leftover food is scraped onto the top plate, leading to some colourful combinations. Urgh.

Although not seen at the time, the mature explanation of these duties is to give a general appreciation towards the kitchen staff and their job rather than creating a social divide, hence the emphasis upon the reason for the chore is to help whomever has to clean up after us.

Anyway, I had better run and find my tutor group in room E for 8:30 a.m. or will be in trouble.

Lessons and Other Such Stuff

Stop! Upon leaving the dining hall, progress is temporarily halted by a bottleneck of people in the corridor. Everyone is feverishly trying to squash through for an invisible goal. It transpires that there are four long tables lined up by the window holding the gold dust that is POST! Each house is designated a separate table for members of that house to have their post displayed and every morning involves a scramble to see if there is anything exciting from home. This takes the form of: letters, cards and sometimes a caring relative will send a tuck parcel (the presence of such an object obviously indicates someone must have been complaining about the food). Newspapers can be ordered and are to be collected by the post, so then at least you can always get something! (*Irrational though it may seem, post, just like Valentine's cards, does provide great excitement!*)

The rush continues onto the tutor group room that we were all told about during the afternoon tea on Sunday. Everyone congregates in the classroom (Room E) where we (roughly twenty-five of us) sit on chairs/tables and wait for a jolly Mr. Coward (no doubt humming a Mozart descant or trombone impression and sympathetically addressing people's questions with a "What is it, my old fruit?") to call out the register that we just have to answer "Here" to.

At 8:40 a.m. there is a blazer check (i.e. a casual glance around the room to make sure that everyone is wearing a blazer) before being ushered along the corridor to the Great Hall for assembly. Sixth form Wardens line the sides of the corridor and have a beady eye on the mobile mass of pupils walking through to the hall, telling several people to, "Pull your socks up please." It is obviously a familiar call due to the set voice that the Wardens used so much that the voices merge into a chorus.

Some of the wardens loved this duty and the evil glint in their eye hinted that they would love to make people do more things than that and we should bring back the days when sixth form could give out punishments, then you'd be in for it. Others just look a bit bored with saying the same line five days a week whilst most just got on with it as though it was the normal part of everyday life that it is. If somebody ignores them, shall we call it "not heard," the offender will get summoned back down the corridor until they pulled their socks up.

With blazer on and socks pulled up to the elbow, we file into the nearest side entrance to the hall in complete silence and collect a hymnbook off the shelves that are fixed onto the wall. The first form takes their place in the first few rows at the front nearest to the stage and each tutor sits (with their graduation gown on) at the end of the rows. The next stage is run so smoothly it has a regimented appearance.

After a short pause, the side of the hall door is opened by the Prime Warden and the Deputy Prime Warden (two sixth forms who get to wear a medal that is passed down from one generation of Wardens to another), who then proceed to hold the door open for the Head Mistress to sweep in and walk up the stairs to the centre of the stage. The appearance of the Prime Warden is the cue for the entire school to stand up so that they are on their feet for the arrival of the Head Mistress.

Assembly is now in full swing and is kicked off with a hymn, sung with the help of the school choir and grand piano that are situated at the back of the hall. Fortunately, the first words that the Head speaks are: "Please be seated."

The Head then proceeds to impart a gem of Christian wisdom to us all before finishing off the assembly by reading the notices. Notices are given to the Head before she walks into assembly and are usually about sports practices that will take place later that day. If there is nothing to be said, the official line to finish off the assembly is: "There are no notices today." This marks the standing up of the speaker, followed by the whole school rising to its feet as the Head leads the Prime Warden out of the door. Nobody can escape yet because the wardens stand at the end of each row and dismiss people a row at a time to avoid a mass squashing of the first years.

Without any time to lose, we consult our timetable and follow the group to the Latin room, amazingly, we manage to find it and still be on time. The room is quite traditional in its layout of desks for two people facing the blackboard in typical exam room style. Everyone takes a seat but upon the appearance of our first teacher we are quiet and rise to our feet, as is expected of us. A thin Irish lady greets us and asks to pick up a textbook and exercise book en route to our seats. She introduces herself as Mrs. Clements and chats for a bit to make sure that we are not too scared by her.

There is no more time to be wasted, so the lesson begins. Here goes.

So now we have our gleaming orange textbooks about Caecillius and his family and we all await the traditional tables of declensions and rote learning: *"amo, amass, amat, amamus, amatis, amant etc."* in typically serious 1950s style. As Mrs. Clements reads the first couple of pages and explains the delights of what a nominative and accusative is, it seems to be adhering to this plan, when suddenly the story turns to the dog called Cerberus. As it does so, Mrs. Clements pushes her reading glasses to the top of her head, jumps onto her desk on all fours and barks without any self-consciousness at all, to illustrate that Cerberus is the pet featured in the story. This is looking up.

Everyone is desperate to giggle but tries very hard to suppress it and fails miserably! Before any more amateur dramatics, the buzzer goes and we are dismissed, leaving Mrs. Clements to disembark from the table.

Its time for morning break, so there is a crush to the dining hall for biscuits and tea. The tea bags are budget ones so they are often left to stew. There is a strict limit of twenty minutes for break so it is quite lucky that we are limited to a small cup of tea/juice/coffee and two biscuits but only the first in the queue get the chocolate ones.

The day continues in a little haze of gathering new textbooks, getting lost around the many corridors and trivial tasks such as putting name and form on a locker in the "underground." The underground is a space where there are rows of small tin lockers that are underneath the classrooms in quite a badly lit and bare area, it is certainly one of those places that are excluded from the open day show round!

At 4:00, the buzzer sounds to signal the end of the day and everyone is free to do their own thing before prep at 4:45 p.m. Well, that is normally what happens, but the house mistress had told us to meet in the hall of Andies after lessons but she did not specify what for.

As it transpires, it is compulsory for all first years to be given a show round to ensure that they know where all the fire escapes are. Good point really. Andies has a fairly unique design in the way that an extra fire escape is built into each dorm. The balcony has a square trap door that can be lifted up to reveal a narrow metal ladder that has been fixed to the wall and only stops upon reaching the trapdoor of the floor below. Due to the fire regulations that specify that everyone has to know where the escape routes are, we had a great time trying out the ladders from the top of house to the bottom but had to stop trying to ambush each other mid-ladder for fear of giving the house mistress a heart attack.

At 4:45, we were allowed off prep for the evening since it was our first day and we do not have any work to do. This means that we were free to just chill out for a bit with each other in the rec and watch TV for a while. Ah, this is the life.

Food and Indigestion

The next morning rolls lazily on and we are fitting into the routine that finds us at breakfast again. Everything happens as it did yesterday including the same routines of the staff walk down and a first year collecting "stuff." Suddenly the tranquillity is broken and fast-paced, suppressed movement and anxiety begins to run from the end of the dining hall in a Mexican wave style. What is going on? This is becoming a familiar question, so the answer is to watch everyone else and copy the sixth form.

The main focus is on the frantic attainment of a saucer from the centre of the table where they are all stacked up. Nobody can move from their chair without any real cause so, to create the minimal amount of obvious disruption, the people in the centre of the table pass the saucers in large piles to either end of the table. It is now plain to see that all of the white teacups in the hall now have matching saucers. The other strange happening is that people have put their bacon sandwiches on a plate and are eating them with a knife and fork. Why the change and why does everyone else always seem to know?

The question is about to be answered by the arrival of a petite, stern-looking lady who has risen from the Head's Chair on High and has begun to walk around each table. She has a hawk-like set of eyes that deliver a withering glare to each person she is examining, this happened to be just about everyone.

The whispered explanation from the neighbouring second years is that this new experience is indeed common and is known as "saucer check." It is to ensure that correct table manners are adhered to, i.e. no chewing gum, eat sandwiches with a knife and fork, a cup is only utilised with a saucer, knife is held properly, napkins are in place and a separate knife has been used for the butter and the jam (any prep that people are trying to do under the table for the first lesson is also discretely hidden).

The sixth formers say that Ms. Tanner, for that is the name of the formidable lady, is actually really nice and will respect you as long as you respect her. Right now I shall just obey. She has a reputation for delivering creative punishments that everyone tries to avoid. A well-known example is that one person was late for breakfast (obviously not realising that the nice kitchen staff will let you walk through the back way) and the offender's punishment was to weed the amphitheatre with a dining fork everyday for twenty minutes before breakfast for a week. Nobody is late when Ms. Tanner is on duty.

Fortunately, today everyone seems to have been prepared, so she strides back to High without any victim. We are now free to go.

Lunchtime whizzes round again but it is such a fundamental part of school life it deserves it's own special section. Have you ever felt that your school food was the worst inedible stodge ever to be seen? There are always three choices at lunch: salad bar, vegetarian and something hot. That needs rephrasing to salad, served with "extra protein" such as crunchy lettuce a la greenfly... School food has become a standing joke for millions of hungry school children nationwide.

It seems to be most cruel that lunch is at 1:00 after simply hours of lessons and your stomach has been making telltale noises that disrupt the class since at least an hour previously. It is always on these hungriest of days that, just before the lunchtime bell, every single lesson can be turned to discussions about exotic food, and just before drooling, you have to remind yourself that you are in school, about to have the delights of school lunches and are not at the local Mc Donald's.

Getting to lunch involves two important stages: walking briskly (always better not to run because no doubt it will be straight into a teacher - not advisable) to the dining hall and then facing the dreaded, the unpredictable, queue. As you become carried along on the wave of people moving en masse, everyone converges with the same aim in mind: how to be the first in the...l o n g...queue.

Just before entering the double doors to the dining hall and delivering a self-congratulatory pat on the back, it is a good idea to practice a game of teacher avoidance or else there is a possibility that the teacher will beckon you aside to discuss what can now be regarded as rather petty course work. If this happens, it will only mean that the next few minutes are spent trying to look remotely interested in coursework whilst maintaining a fixed smile that masques disappointment as one eye discretely watches all of the people file past. The certain knowledge at this stage that you are in for the scrapings of greasy food that line the bottom of the pans reduces the appetite.

So, now the position is at the back of the queue that curves round every table and door in sight. The tactic now is one that requires smoothness; look for any friends further up the queue and start talking to them and they will try to fit you into a space with them.

(*Over time, the practice of queue barging is conditioned out of people at school because it is deemed to be rude, besides, the sixth form privilege allows them to walk straight to the front of the queue.*)

Now is the time to be served—hurrah! Unfortunately, the food has run out so I have to resort to the salad bar. A new box of cottage cheese is opened, and lo and behold, it has become a fertile mineral for the development of microbes. Clearly the cheese will be thrown away. Nope, after a few seconds thought, the penicillin is mixed vigorously into the cheese and served to unsuspecting people.

A quick look at the meat pie confirms the suspicion that the "meat" occasionally contains blood vessels. Right, moving onto dessert. Custard. The skin is sooo thick that it is two shades darker than whatever is underneath. The joy of having something on the plate is soon dashed when the cold, lumpy custard surrounded by rubbery skin will not make its way from plate to mouth.

At this point, the hand bell is rung from High Table and the whole dining hall ceases to eat (!) and are silent whilst the notices are read out. After this the plates are cleared away quickly so the alternative to hunger is to slip an apple into the blazar pocket without anybody seeing because eating outside of the dining hall is strictly forbidden. Once safely out of sight it can be consumed, making the grand total of the gourmet lunch being...one apple. Ah well, fruit is considered to be healthy eating.

Prep

Hurrah! The 4:00 buzzer signals the end of a day's lessons. The time period between now and 4:45 p.m. is affectionately known as "four o'clock." The members of staff get to eat cakes served to them on silver platters in the staff room without any interruptions from us lot! Prep begins at 4:45 down in the school classrooms. It is split into two halves of forty-five minutes with half an hour for tea at 5:30 p.m. but until then we are free to do whatever we like. The first thing is to change into home clothes, ah, it's great to be back in jeans.

(It should be noted that people are able to wear anything they like without anybody raising an eyebrow because it would be considered bad form to insult somebody's taste in clothes)

At 4:40 p.m. up at house, the hand bell is rung and everyone is kicked out of the rec (*large living room*) whilst desperately trying to set the video recorder to tape "Neighbours" and "Home and Away." This happens every night so that we can all squash into the rec at 6:45 p.m. after prep and not miss out on the trials and tribulations of Ramsey Street.

There is a huge rush to go back to the classrooms to be on time for the register but there are the usual stragglers that get ushered down to school by the house mistresses. Each person is designated a place in separate rooms that have a mix of the first four years in the school. The sixth formers are on a rota so that there is one member of the Lower Sixth who has to "babysit" the people in the room for a week at a time. It is their responsibility to take the register and maintain silence but there is always a member of staff patrolling between the rooms. The only flaw in the plan is when the sixth former becomes a little bored and starts to talk to anyone who wants to respond…

The fifth formers are lucky enough to be put into Room S (study room) and have no supervision because they are deemed to be responsible enough. Any sixth formers not on the rota can stay up at house (Stanley's) and are left to do their own thing. (*This system reflects the usual idea that the younger years are disciplined into doing "correct" behaviour, but more freedom and respect is given to the more senior years.*)

During prep it is possible to be excused and go to the music rooms in order to practice your instrument that you have private lessons on (the music teachers love you for doing this and will beam at anyone they recognise). The practice rooms are based in a separate wing of the school. There are several small, rectangular rooms (relatively soundproof but you may find yourself competing with Mozart being played on the piano, a violin, cello and perhaps a late voice lesson) for people to practice whichever instrument they have but there is usually a piano in each room. Although there is a surplus of pianos, the thing to guard jealously is a really smart music stand that can stand up straight. In the harp room, the music stand is actually hidden out of sight of preying eyes, otherwise, it will no doubt be "borrowed."

When the borders go to tea, the day girls catch the school buses to go home. Tea is a really informal affair in the dining hall but the staff can eat together in their separate dining room where they are waited on. We finish eating quite quickly and decide to go and explore the long, dark corridors of the school. This suddenly changes into a game of hide and seek where people have to be careful to duck below the windows so as not to give themselves away.

The second half of prep is not very relevant to the first years because we don't get that much work to do—yay! Apparently, the second years can get up to eight pieces of prep a night, urgh!

6:45: End of prep. For now, it's back up to house. Time to eat pasta and toast (there are never enough knives to butter toast, so the back of a spoon is just as good) and talk in each other's rooms or group on the floor in the corridor.

It's not over yet…

Saturday School

The routine is very similar today but with one vital difference: half an hour lie in due to there being no assemblywoohoo! Every Saturday there is a short school day of three hours from 9am until noon. It is a fairly laid-back affair for first years with the lessons not having a tough academic basis. First up are presentation skills. (*Although not recognised by the first form for many years to come, presentation and drama skills are given great emphasis in school and these lessons are just the start. Pupils can take private drama lessons and progress through the London Academy of Music and Dramatic Arts (LAMDA) grades or wait until the sixth form when it is compulsory to take the English Speaking Board Exam*)

Mr. Jones hands us a short scenario that we have to study in groups of four. The case study is that we have to imagine that we are a catering company and we will have to present our proposal for a wedding plan and convince the couple that they should choose our company to cater for their big day whilst adhering to the budget. Now we have thirty minutes to compose a company: name, location, niche market and catering plan to catch the couple's attention. It's fairly simple to split people up into what they want to do so we just get on with it.

Thirty minutes later…

We all return to the main room at the allotted time and wait our turn to deliver our short presentation, using signs as props, without a hitch. Mr. Jones stands thoughtfully at the front of the class, rubbing his chin. He announces the winner to be…another team. (Gasp.) A round of applause ensues whilst the winners go up to the front of the class to collect their prize of chocolate. We are all told to hush whilst Mr. Jones announces his reasons for selecting that particular team:

"In this country many people are impressed by a particular image that they think is professional. A London address is a way to impress and a second point is to set the price at a slightly higher level than the budget because a higher price is linked with better quality, it's our big day so we are going to splash out on the company that we think is going to produce the best results."

Lesson learnt.

All off to the sports hall for a leisurely couple of hours of hockey and lax to finish off Saturday school for this week. Or so we think. The sports staff had decided otherwise. They wanted to make "proper" use of the two hours not followed by any lessons to press the termly torture of "The Long Cinder" upon us. A humorous Howellian obviously accurately named the cinder many generations ago and the name has stuck.

The compulsory cross country that goes up and down two miles of hills strikes fear into the heart of everyone bar the masochistic amongst us. There is no escape, that is something we are all reminded of because the three members of staff will take a car and place themselves behind bushes at the most difficult parts of the course where they will hide SAS style whilst waiting for their unsuspecting prey to finish having a cardiac at the top of the hill before jumping out and, for example, yelling: "Hurry, Kelly, stop walking! All of the lunch will have gone by the time you cross the finishing line!"

With this, ahem, encouragement, Kelly persists in jogging until reaching the corner and once (hopefully) out of sight, subsequently hugs onto a tree for support. The dilemma really begins though as she realises that in an attempt to shortcut, she has gone through some soggy grass and curses as her trainer gets glued into the mud where it stubbornly remains. Nope, there will really be no lunch left today.

Although she is talented in many areas, including art and music, sport and Kelly's laid-back approach to getting to places never really jelled. It was only earlier in the week that, after being late getting changed back into uniform after sports for a French lesson, the teacher had told her that she was unacceptably late and she will have to time herself, repeatedly changing into and out of her sports kit so that she will be able to attend French lessons on a Wednesday at the same time as everybody else. Oops.

41

With that over and as the sun begins to shine, we can do what we like to entertain ourselves, and since we are not allowed outside of the school gates all week, passing through the gates is the one activity we all want to do. It was policy until last year that first and second years had to walk up the hill to the shops in small groups whilst being accompanied by a house mistress to keep us all in order. The problem with this was that there was a serious restraint on when people could move anywhere, so the rules have been relaxed just in time for us—yay!

However, there are still guidelines that we must observe. We have to "sign out" (write what we are doing in a book in the duty room) up at house to say where we are going (we are allowed from the newsagents at the bottom of the hill to the chippie at the end of the street), who we are venturing out with and an expected time of return. The minimum number of each party has to be three. The theory behind this is that if one of us hurts ourselves then there are enough people for one to stay with the injured party whilst the other person gets help.

This week, in the evening, there is not much to do apart from chilling in the house rec with everyone else and a video, not forgetting the essential tub of chocolate ice cream. The problem with being a first year is that the seats are split in a hierarchy from the fifth form downwards. The eldest girls in the room are the lucky souls who get to sit on the comfy sofa in front of the TV, and if somebody more senior to them enters the rec, they will offer to surrender their seat, but this is usually (but not always) politely declined. As a first year, we end up sitting on the hard-backed chairs, straining over the heads of the people in front. Ah well, we will get our turn.

Later on in the evening, someone will do the "toast round" where they take orders from the room for toast with chocolate spread/jam etc. and will bring it in rounds. In the meantime, the video is stopped until everyone can watch it. 'Tis a nice community feel.

11:00: Lights Out

The Day of Rest

Sunday is the traditional day of rest, but not for us. All of the first years are ushered downstairs twenty minutes earlier than everyone else to make sure that our shoes are polished and we look immaculately dressed in formal uniform. Pages from newspapers are scattered on the duty room floor so that we can make a non-permanent mess whilst cleaning our shoes.

This morning it is off to the school church for a morning service. It is evensong every other weekend so that is the time we have a lie in for as long as we like and breakfast up at house—yay!

Each house prepares to walk to church together, so everyone has to be ready with cloaks on, the threat being that we might not need them now but we sure will once we get into church.

The school church is an ornate building just ten minute's walk through the school grounds. As we go through the church door in single file, it is gravely silent, bar the welcoming tunes on the organ. St. Andrew's house members have to walk to the right of the church and sit down in the rows of polished wooden seats that are below our house banner.

Each house has its own banner featuring the corresponding house badge sewn onto it, hung periodically spaced throughout the church. The first years have to sit in the front row of each house's section and have a house mistress on either end of the row to keep an eye on us. Once everyone is seated, the choir walk down the aisle to the choir stalls in a line of pairs led by the head of the choir who carries a metre long, gold cross upright ahead of them. Each member of the choir holds their music inside a hard backed burgundy folder with the school crest emblazoned on the front in gold that they carry with the crest shown towards the congregation.

It is very prestigious being in the choir, especially since they recorded a CD. The choir is made up of pupils between the third and sixth form who have passed an audition. Occasionally a person has thought that they have been unfairly rejected so they have gone to see Mr. Jones to express their disdain, consequently, they have been allowed into the choir as a reward for having the courage to push themselves forward.

The choir rehearses three times a week and performs at all of the end of term services as well as at the weekly church service.

The service continues in the usual format of hymns (we each have a copy of the school hymnbook placed in the holder of the chair in front of us; the hymnbooks are the same description as the choir's folders) followed by a reading and a sermon. There is a rota for the Bible reading that includes every border, so it means that everyone reads an extract at some point during the year. The readers sit on the very front row and walk up to the golden eagle lectern at the correct point dictated in the order of service.

Twenty-five minutes into the service…

Golly, it's getting cold. They only put the heating on when the parents are here for the end of term services. It's amazing how I cannot feel my toes but being cold is the only thing that I can think about. *Must keep looking ahead like everyone else and concentrate on what the reverend is talking about.*

"And on the seventh day…"

It's still cold. Nope, it is not working. Suddenly a mutual look at the person next to me reveals that they are thinking the same thing. This is the worst thing that can happen as a smirk turns into a grin, this turns into smouldered giggles. Oh no, both of us try to look at the floor, ceiling, chair, in fact, at anywhere but at each other because that would just set us off again. Hisses of warning and glares that foretold of unprecedented punishment travel down the row from the house mistresses. This makes us even worse, but why does laughter have to be unstoppable? Eventually, we get it under control, but we are going to be in for it later.

Sure enough, after the church service and back up at house, whilst the others disperse to get changed, Samantha and I are beckoned into the Duty room. The door is shut behind us. This is the ominous sign that signals to the rest of the house not to disturb the house mistresses.

There is a panel of the two house mistresses who have a fixed look that is incredibly disapproving and invite us to sit down. The reverend is seated in the comfy chair and has been softened by a mug of tea (bet she was cold too). The senior house mistress begins by asking us to explain why we think we are here, why we were laughing and then saying how rude it all was. She also went to great lengths to say how disrespectful it was to the reverend, at this point we promptly apologised.

Our punishment was to write a letter of apology to the reverend and the rest would be up to her. The reverend seemed quite pleased with this and then let us go. Phew.

It is an open secret that someone in the fifth form actually manages to take their walkman into church and hide it underneath their cloak to pass the time, fortunately for them, they manage to get away with it! (*Nobody would ever dob anyone in for doing things they are not meant to, so that is how they escape undetected*)

The rest of the day typically follows a lazy fashion. After a full roast lunch, there is free time to be filled with anything one likes, including: swimming in the outdoor pool, going uptown, prep or just chilling with everyone. It is possible to sign up for other various activities such as a short course in windsurfing or canoeing so it's up to the individual.

The day passes on until tea at 5:00 p.m. The house mistresses always take a leisurely supper in their staff dining room because it is their chance to chat to other adults instead of us lot! It means that we have to wait for them to finish up at house before they unlock house again. It could result in us waiting at the back entrance (staff and sixth form only are allowed through the front door). The way round this problem has been perfected over generations and the solution is to leave a small window open in the second floor bathroom. Running up the side of the house is a fat metal drainpipe just asking to be climbed. The usual plan is for someone to shimmy up the drainpipe and crawl through the window before opening the door from the inside. The house mistresses never actually find out how we manage to get into a locked building.

The day is ours again until the house bell rings at roughly 7:00 p.m. to signal the beginning of the house meeting. It is important that everyone arrives promptly so that a register can be taken by the Head of House before they then inform the house mistresses that we are ready for their arrival.

Although the meeting is in the second rec with the comfy chairs and is rather informal, we all stand up when they enter and have the best chairs set out in the front of the room for the house mistresses to sit down on.

The meeting follows the format of a short agenda of house activities and we are reminded that it is now possible to sign up for a course in windsurfing. The highlight of the meeting is that we have to get some ideas together for Dorm Decs. Thankfully, this is explained for our benefit. It is a Christmas tradition where the whole dorm is transformed into a theme of the individual dorm's choice, ready for the celebrations at the end of term.

The meeting is rounded up by the mention of "any other business" (AOB), and the house mistresses exit the room first, leaving us all free and ready to face another week…

Christening In

Week 2

It is time to be a "proper" initiated member of St. Andrew's or I will not be able to call myself an Andyite in the eyes of everyone. The process of "Christening In" has been shrouded in mystery and has been hinted at in name only since the beginning of term. The timing of the procedure is up to the dorm head so it could be a few weeks into term, just when you think that you have escaped... but they have far too much fun to ever forget about it.

History:

"Christening In" is a tradition that is almost as old as the school. In fact, it has been around for so long the house mistresses got to know about it and decided that they would put their foot down and the practice would cease that very day. But it continued. It is now done after lights out and carried out as quietly as possible within the dorm, the only light being what shines through the window in the main dorm door.

Suppose I had better tell you what on earth all the fuss is about. It used to be that first years had to undergo certain trials to be completely accepted into Andies but anybody who joined later than the first year had the privilege of being exempt. The reason it was banned was because the house mistresses heard that pupils were made to run naked around house and back to the dorm. It was initially supposed to happen in the dark but the cruel dorm head, in that particular instance, flashed the lights on just to terrify the first year.

Tip: Refuse to do this in no uncertain terms (unless its your thing) or the gleeful dorm head will push anybody into it just for the entertainment value. Respect is given to confidence in daring to stand up to everyone in the dorm.

After flatly refusing to do the recounted tale, the other form of "Christening In" that is offered is more in line with the familiar Christian service involving water. This starts to sound better but the revelations do not stop there because, horror of horror, as the animated faces of the rest of the dorm situated round the cubi take great joy in imparting, it is (quite unbelievably but I'm afraid that they mean it) none other than toilet water. There is much tormenting discussion as to whether the water is going to be clean or dirty…(please please let this be a joke).

The next great decider is which lucky person gets to use their mug to scoop the water out of the dorm loo. As usual, the task is delegated to the youngest people in the hierarchy in the dorm. The two second years huddle hunched up in conspiratorial whispers as they leave the dorm, shutting the door behind them and squabbling through squeaks of, "Urgh, no!" over which mug it is going to be.

There is almost silence now with the exception of the cackles of the second years emanating from the dorm toilet. There might be noise but the thought of, *Damn, how do I get out of this one?* tends to be a little distracting. It all seems to be spiralling out of control as there is no recollection of actually agreeing to this one.

Think logically: what are the options? Could always refuse again but then it would be a bit of a spoilsport who didn't join in. After all, it is not going to be life threatening or even hurt, it's just gross. Chances are they would have chosen clean water because who would want dirty toilet water to be used in their mug? They wouldn't, would they?

The other option, seemingly more and more acceptable (especially as the second years keep walking over to the sink and filling it with water from the mug over and over again), is to just run away and tell the house mistress everything, but that would just be dobbing people in, unfortunately, that simply can't be done. Hmmm…

The options seem to have run out. It's getting jolly close to crunch time and images of the need for deep cleansing for the next six years are becoming more and more real. Then, as if by the grace of God, the hand bell is rung vigorously outside of the dorm, there is plenty of running around from other dorms, and added to the din is a shrill whistle and the warning of "Fire!" Yes! It's a fire practice. Hurrah! This gives some plotting time.

The whole house is timed to make sure that Andies has been evacuated within a time limit so that, according to theory, should a fire occur, we wouldn't die. Everyone has to line up in their year groups on the stone quad between the houses whilst their names are read from the register. The whole register has to be finished before the dithering bodies (British Winter night, remember) are allowed to disperse but it is not cold that provides the motivation this time. Nope, the opportunity to run back to the dorm is now, whilst the older years are strolling and talking to each other, no doubt exchanging stories about terrorising the first years.

Lizzy (the other first year) has had a similar idea, and upon bursting into the dorm at such a speed that I almost ran into a wall, she is found lifting the plug whilst rapidly beckoning me to keep watch for the others returning. If I did see the others, what was I meant to do? It might look a tad suspicious to say, "Sorry, but nobody can enter because I say so."

Anyway, I stand guard whilst Lizzy puts the tap on at full speed to fill the sink again. Why, oh why, does the tap look like it is dripping one stubborn drip after another? That done, we run backwards through the door and hang around in the corridor and enter the room at the same time as the first person in the dorm returns. Mission accomplished.

All that is needed now is to act disgusted at going near the pure water (drama lessons are never in vain). A quick dipping of fingers into the water to create a figure of the cross on the forehead and the process is over but the rest of the dorm is not finished yet. Oh no, what could they be thinking of next? Any smugness at foiling the first test is beginning to lose its glory. The second, third and fourth years go to the back of the dorm and whisper their next plot.

They don't emerge until fifteen minutes later when two of them casually stroll into our cubi and put a small bundle of things onto a bed. The little parcel is not recognisable in the dim light but they use a piece of paper and start to roll powder up in it. Ah, now it makes sense. They begin to try to persuade us to take drugs but not being all that bothered about potentially dying with a possible abnormal reaction, the only option is to maintain a neutral face and act as though it is the most normal and well thought of thing in the world.

Eventually, they can keep up their act no longer and roll around in fits of laughter. They explain how they had just crushed up nothing other than a packet of polo mints and had to stop because they could not bring themselves to continue and try to inhale them! Apparently, they just wanted to test our reaction and we both passed the test. What did we do? Ah well, let's not dwell on it, yay, the "Christening In" is over! Now we can participate in the house games as an Andyite and wear our house badges with pride.

Duties
The survival guide for bemused first years
(Who does what)

Well, after the honeymoon period of the first week, it's time to get acquainted with what you are expected to do. Oh yes, do not forget your responsibilities, so here they are in time old tradition:

Year——Duty——Pardon?

1st——Laundry——Sort out the huge piles of uniform and unpaired socks that belong to individuals in the whole house after the weekly load has returned from the internal laundry. Name places are set in alphabetical order around a spare room at the back of house so that the first years can dig out the correct name tape from each item of clothing and put it in the corresponding pile. It is done at 4:00 every Thursday.

1st & 2nd——Bells——A hand bell that is rung early every morning by one person who has been put on a rota. The duty is to ring the first and third bell, on time, outside each of the four dorms and the fifth form rooms. The house mistress rings the second bell to enable the person to madly rush to get dressed. Making someone do bells is a favourite punishment for anyone caught dorm hopping so that could give one a couple of days off a week.

1ˢᵗ——Clearing——Join part of the tradition that dictates that first years have to stack all of the plates at the lunch table and carry them to the kitchen. It involves scraping all of the left over food onto the top plate. Clearing is dubbed a privilege because it is joining in an old, old tradition. (*One day the first years staged a rebellion - encouraged by none other than Mr, Jones - but soon discovered the wrath of social pressure! Not doing your bit is unthinkable.*)

1ˢᵗ——Spread——An old plastic bucket has been given the sacred title of "spread bucket." The bucket is collected by one first year, again, on a rota basis, every evening from the dining hall. It contains two loaves of bread and spread, e.g. jam, peanut butter and chocolate spread. This duty is the most important because, otherwise, two many dorm mates will be hungry. A first year has often been seen to run down to school to pick it up at the last minute.

2ⁿᵈ——Bins——The bins in the dorm have to emptied daily into a large bin bag that is then put into the bins at the back of house.

Other information:
Another favourite punishment.
Done on a rota.

3ʳᵈ——Chairs——Clear the breakfast tables and then pull the chairs out far enough from the tables to enable the kitchen staff easy access to clean underneath the tables.

Head of House——Write all of the rotas. Check that everyone is happy.

Games

The Definitive Guide

This is what makes boarding worthwhile! Now that we are initiated into Andies, we can join in properly. The first game had been pre-arranged as a coordinated effort by all four dorm heads for that night to take place after all of the first years had been christened in. It is an important tradition to pass down the games to each new generation of first years, so here goes!

The customary format is that "Moo" is played first twice or continued until the housemistresses take notice then it is followed by a round of "Farting Rocks" or "Mattress Sliding." "Packti Races" are usually reserved for Sunday afternoons or spare time after prep whilst "Dorm Hopping" is just an everyday occurrence.

Moo

All of the dorms on a particular floor do this at the same time and each floor alternates to create the maximum noise. Moo is a stampede of everyone on the floor as they run through the fire doors onto the central landing whilst making the noise of a farm animal at the top of their voices, so there is a mixture of oink, moo and baa. People stay on the landing, making their animal's noise for a twenty second period before rushing back to their respective dorms. When there is silence once more, it is the cue for the other floor to have their turn.

The whole process continues until one unlucky dorm bursts through the fire doors to encounter the house mistress walking up the stairs. This sighting results in a sharp about turn and people rushing into each other as they are going in opposite directions until the message spreads to the end of the group. The task is now to dive into bed (hopefully your own, but this does not always happen) and pull the duvet over your head whilst lying still and pretending to be sound asleep as though you have been there since lights out. Strangely enough, this tactic does not always fool the house mistress. She walks into the silent room slowly so that the door opens creak by creak. The full dorm lights are put on and she says sternly:

"Now, girls, we shall have no more of this. If I have to come up again tonight, you will all have a suitable punishment."

When she is satisfied and has safely gone out of the way, there are a few stirrings akin to nocturnal animals that sniff the air to test for predators before emerging from their den. The game now changes course to "Farting Rocks" to lend a little anonymity…

Farting Rocks

This again takes place on the central landing between the two dorms on each floor. Each person wraps themselves in their duvet so that they are completely covered from head to toe and they then roll into a human ball on the floor. The game is most effective just after Moo if the house mistresses have not yet made their way upstairs because they will do so shortly. The idea is that Moo has attracted their attention so that when the house mistresses appear they can only guess the likely names of people, but when one's name is mentioned, the person whom is referred to has to make a loud farting noise.

Usually the house mistress will give up and go back to the duty room for a coffee and will just wake the entire dorm up thirty minutes early.

Mattress Sliding

Great fun! First of all, the location of the house mistresses has to be found out because it would not look good if they unexpectedly walked out of a dorm to discover people holding a plain mattress (try explaining that one!). The game involves removing a spare mattress from a disused single room (reserved for fifth form and to move people into as a punishment) and using all of the force of six people to drag it up to the top of the stairs whilst two others stand at the bottom of the stairs as a look out. It is also important to prop open the fire door on the landing to facilitate an easy getaway should we all need to run.

Once at the top of the flight of stairs, four people cram onto the mattress in a straight line and hold onto each other for dear life whilst simultaneously pushing off with their feet, it actually works incredibly well. Everyone rotates so that people get a go at the front and the back of the mattress and take their turn as look out.

Sometimes there is a suppressed signal from the people on guard that a house mistress has been spotted
through the mirror that kick starts rushed panic! The four people hop off the mattress and everyone drags the (seemingly increasingly) heavy mattress through the fire door and back into the spare room before rushing back into either the dorm or the kitchen. The whole process begins later with people becoming more daring and sliding on the mattress face down.

Packti Races

This is possible due to the close proximity of packtis (wardrobes) and cupboards. The aim is to climb from one end of the dorm to the other only using the packtis and surfaces raised off the floor because nobody is allowed to touch the carpet, as this would be cheating. Normally, there is enough stuff to climb over to allow two people to race.

Not a bad way to spend Sunday afternoon.

Dorm Hopping

As usual, this only occurs after lights out. It is the name for visiting friends in other dorms, and since any movement between floors has to be done silently in the dark, it takes quite a skill to master. The corner mirrors on the landing are handy for spotting any house mistresses who might be waiting on the stairs but the heavy slam of the fire doors is the most dangerous giveaway. Once actually in the dorm, there is a back up to prevent any detection in the form of being able to hide between the clothes and shoes in a packti, but whatever you do, don't stand up because the big clang and crash of head meets clothes hangers is a bit of a giveaway and the house mistress will not be particularly amused.

The punishment for persistent offenders is to be moved into one of the spare single rooms for the night. The only problem with this idea is that it only succeeds in more dorm hopping as people in the dorm will go and visit the person so that they will not get lonely.

Christmas Celebrations

This term finishes with many quirky, fun events. There is Head's Party complete with staff pantomime, dorm decs followed by carols round the tree in House and a midi (midnight feast) the night before the End of Term Service that is held in the school church.

One month to the Christmas holiday…

Dorm Decs

The planning for the celebrations, for us, begins several weeks in advance of the end of term with the planning of dorm decs. First of all, a theme has to be decided and then a design that involves all of the room has to be made so we have a post-lights-out meeting in the fourth years' cubies at the back of the dorm to decide what to do. The fund for paints and materials has been donated by parents from the beginning of term and is split equally between the four dorms.

The aim is that everyone gets involved in the whole process and are only given tasks that they are capable of doing. Our dorm theme is going to be Heaven and Hell but we have no idea what the other dorms are up to simply because it is all kept as a secret from each other.

Soon afterwards, the painting of sheets of paper to cover the walls begins and they are left to dry whilst strewn all over the dorm so it becomes an art form to step anywhere. What usually happens is that it is easier to carry a paintbrush and quickly brush over any shoe prints before anybody notices. Gradually gravestones are made from cardboard and put around the cubi whilst the packtis are covered in paper that is shaped like a coffin.

Over a period of a few weeks the decorations are taking shape but props are kept hidden from view. The aim of the decorations is that the cubies are turned into a 3D version of the theme and the people who sleep in the cubies dress up to act as characters that suit the theme.

One week to the end of term…

The finished product is shown to teachers who walk around each dorm and judge a winner to be announced later that evening at the Carols Round the Tree ceremony.

The last minute touches are added too "Hell" so that there is straw for bedding (all traces of everyday living are removed, usually to be pushed into the packti) and moldy bread is left lying on the side cupboards. Silhouette images of tortured people have been stuck in the background. The live models are dressed in prisoner's clothes and lie groaning on the wooden base of the school beds that have been sprinkled with straw.

In contrast, "Heaven" has mellow music playing, is decorated in the style of a monastery with candles and smiling people. The small entranceway between the front of the dorm and the back half has been transformed into the Pearly Gates.

After the judges have been round, we are allowed to have a look at what other people have done. Word soon gets round about who has won, although how we all know is a bit of a mystery since nobody is allowed to move from their positions until everybody has looked around the whole house. The winning dorm has done Hollywood studios.

Each cubi had been changed to look like the set from a recent film and a pre-recorded tape talks people around the scene.

Back downstairs, the next entertainment is commencing…

Carols Around the Tree
The second rec has been altered earlier in the day so that there are plenty of seats for the staff to watch the stage that comprises of the space left at the front of the room. The room has been given a Christmas feel by the presence of a large, decorated fir tree in the corner of the room.

Tonight is the chance to perform fun pieces of music (usually piano) or drama. People in the house have prepared several individual and group performances for the audience. They include drama from private lessons that are either Shakespearean or a contemporary piece, including one of Roald Dahl's unorthodox versions of Cinderella that leaves the audience howling with laughter.

The traditional event continues with all pupils seated on the floor whilst Mr Jones takes his seat at the piano and proceeds to encourage everyone to join in and sing along to all of the well-known Christmas carols. By now it is dark and candles are brought into the room to add to the Christmas feel. After roughly twenty minutes, the judges and Mr Jones have to depart and go to the other houses in order to do the same events there.

Two days before the end of term...

Head's Party

This tradition is as old as the school. It is made up of three main parts: a dinner in the dining hall for the whole school, staff pantomime and a sixth form written and performed play that is based on caricaturing all of the teachers.

For the dinner, we are all allowed to sit with our friends. It is a really fun occasion and people try to wear the most festive decorations, including the obligatory paper hat from the crackers, tinsel, antler headbands etc.

In an unusual twist, the teachers wait on the pupils for the first half of the dinner. This means that they rush around carrying silver platters of Christmas lunch trimmings and try to deliver to all of the tables. In the second half of the dinner, they retreat to "High."

After everyone has stuffed themselves with Christmas pudding, the Head Mistress picks up the bell that sits in front of her. Upon hearing the bell, silence reigns. She then calls for the kitchen staff to emerge from the canteen area and asks them to all stand in a line in full view of everyone. The Head delivers a speech of appreciation to them all then we join her in applauding them for all of their hard work throughout the year. The staff all look delighted although some blush at the attention!

After this, the staff leaves. Naturally, the Head exits first and the rest follow. This is our signal to file into the Great Hall and wait for this year's staff pantomime that has been kept a complete secret.

We all cram into the seats in the Great Hall. The trick is to arrive early or you will be left with the seats that are on the wooden steps at the back of the hall, that means a certain doom of bum ache after forty minutes.

The staff play is introduced as "Cinderella." Extra roles have been written into the play so that everyone gets a part, unless there is a woodcutter that I don't remember. The costumes are perfect for the roles and must have been borrowed from the depths of the costume department. The main suspects for the large roles are of course Mrs. Grey-Lloyd as non other than the title role, along with Mr. Jones who is the strutting Handsome Prince. The end finishes to great acclaim with Mr. Jones actually picking up Mrs. Grey-Lloyd as they dash off stage to be married, and could that be a stocking flashed by Cinders?! This invites a standing ovation from us all and notoriety for the staff in the next edition of the "Howellian" magazine.

The cast dash off to clear the stage in time for the sixth form to make an entrance dressed as a typical image of the teachers. The sketch is a condensed version of a fictional meeting in the staff room whilst the staff are eating afternoon tea. Mr. Coward is pictured as the one with uncontrollable mad-professor-style hair, humming merrily to himself, and has the trademark bulging pockets that are filled with pens and probably a lot of other things that he has forgotten about.

Next sweeps in Mrs. Grey-Lloyd with arms outstretched in front of her to help display a fabulous point like the great orator that she is. The person playing Mr. Jones has filled their stomach area with padding in order to give that "Pavarotti" look, positioned behind Mrs. Grey-Lloyd's back doing a comical, sweat-wiping sweep of the brow as an impression of Mrs. G-L.

In a corner of the room are Mr. Ward, the young physics teacher (dressed in mismatched shades of tie and blazer due to his colour blindness) and a nineteen-year-old Australian girl called Sarah who is helping the house mistresses here as part of her gap year. The two people are positioned on chairs opposite each other. The caricature is of them making flirtatious looks and knee tappings at each other whilst simultaneously looking the other way, absolutely certain that nobody else had noticed.

The night before the end of term…

Midi

The midnight feasts occur at the end of every term as an informal celebration. Each dorm has a separate midnight feast (although sometimes two dorms merge and they invite friends from other dorms to join in) so then they can use the rec for the videos. Each person has to donate a few pounds to pay for the food in the midi, but they get to write a list of three items of chocolate and cake that they would like to eat. The third and fourth years then go up town and buy all of the food for everyone but they also buy food for sandwiches as well.

The four dorm heads decide between them who is going to have their midi on the last night of term. It is a fought over time slot because they can get ruthless revenge on any of the dorms who had played tricks on them previously! Once it is all sorted, the whole thing is meant to be a secret but the house mistresses manage to find out about it but turn a blind eye and respect the termly tradition.

There is serious debate about whether it is better to sleep before and after the midi or whether it is less tiring to stay awake for forty-eight hours. Anyway, at midnight everyone wraps up in their duvets and squashes through the fire doors (without slamming the doors thanks to the skills learnt through dorm hopping) and goes downstairs to the rec.

The fourth years are usually in control of the food and videos whilst the rest of us simply follow along. Once in the rec, it is the fourth years who sit on the comfy sofa in the middle whilst the younger the year you are in, the further away from the best spot you get.

Food is given out whilst the videos are sorted and the lights are turned off to create a better atmosphere (even though sometimes this means that people who are brave enough to move end up standing in a vanilla slice). The videos are usually so scary/violent that when people go to the toilet, they get somebody else to walk out to the corridor in the dark with them.

At about 3:00 am, when enough TV has been watched, it is time to play tricks. Ha, the favourite one is to hide the morning hand bell as revenge for it ringing at 7:20 a.m. all term to wake us up! It is great fun to sneak around the house and do tricks such as putting shoe polish on the toilet seat or fill the toilet cistern with bubble bath so that it erupts in floods of bubbles when it is flushed.

Other dorms anticipate the tricks so there are certain booby traps to deter anyone who wants to get into the actual dorm. A favourite warning signal is to stack as many metal coat hangers behind the dorm's door which are impossible to pass without them clattering. Sometimes a tub of water is balanced on the top of the door (so hopefully it is not opened for the first time by a house mistress in the morning). Upon passing these defenses, there are other problems, particularly because it all happens in the dark. Sellotape is stuck crossing the walkway between the two sides of the dorm in order to catch unsuspecting people like human flypaper. Don't forget the usual rows of pins lying on the floor…

Given how hard it is to enter a dorm that has been done up in the style of Fort Knox, it is much more fun (and less painful) to play at loo papering. This is a really cool, messy game that involves collecting spare rolls of toilet tissue from everywhere in the house. The next step is to unravel it all and soak it in the basin. After this, it is picked up then wrapped around the banisters and dropped down the stairs in a mushy mess. Dry loo rolls can be tied around the outside of the house and finished in a huge bow at the front door.

After this, we return to the dorm but talk until time to get up in the morning because going to sleep for a couple of hours now will really make you tired. Since we are awake before everyone else, we get to run around and wake up the other dorms (this also makes up for hiding the bell).

Then, of course, after letting the loo papering bask in its own glory, we quickly cleared it up before breakfast.

Christmas Church Service

The church service at the end of term is the traditional Christmas service, complete with the nine well known readings, including the famous line that anyone who has ever been to church will know: "And it came to pass in those days that there was a decree in Jerusalem that all the world should be taxed…"

Today calls for Formal Uniform. It really is an art to tie your own bow (it has to have a small, tight tie at the top and have longer ends that dangle down) so whilst we all wait in the tutor groups after breakfast to be led into church, we all check each other's bows.

At around 10:00, two sixth formers move swiftly around the class rooms to tell everyone that it is now time to walk down to church. The Wardens lead each tutor group down to the church at set intervals so that the arrival of the form groups is staggered but the whole year walk silently into the church together in pairs.

The smartly dressed parents are seated in the back section of the church and the bible readers have priority seats on the front row. It is at this stage that the proud parents try to find their daughters and wave at them whilst they sport a broad smile but we have to ignore them as instructed in the carol service rehearsals (the carols and leading in are practised instead of assembly every morning for the last four weeks of term).

Whilst the crowd is assembling, the atmosphere is kept jolly by the tunes on the church organ. The only other noise is the silent hum of whispered conversation from the parents accompanied by the occasional, "Excuse me, can I just get past please?" as everyone fits into the church.

An order of service is handed to people upon entering the church and handily contains the words of all of the hymns. Silence reigns upon the appearance of the school choir at the back of the church. The silence is broken only by the solo, unaccompanied voice of a choir member singing the first verse of "Once In Royal David's City." The beginning of the second verse is the cue for the choir to parade into the church like they do every Sunday.

The service continues in the traditional format of hymns and readings broken only by the modern songs sung by the choir. All of the bible readers stand behind the golden eagle lectern. The Head Mistress reads the last reading, and when she stands up to read, the entire congregation stands up throughout the length of the lesson.

After the service, we are all led out in reverse order of entry and are not allowed to talk until outside of the church grounds. The next stage is to go to the Great Hall.

The kitchen staff have prepared mince pies on silver platters and sherry to celebrate the end of term. This is the opportunity for parents, staff and pupils to mingle and say goodbye until next term…

Easter Term

Life Continues

This is a really fun term with snowball fights, using lax sticks to launch the snow from. Life continues with practice for music exams, concerts, trials for National Youth Orchestra, county trials for sport and inter-house matches. Ooh, don't forget the drama practice. It's normal to hear people being tested on their lines in the corridor up at house.

All in all, stuff is always happening, so it's hard not to join in!

Cold Campaign

Brrrrrrr. Yep, it's definitely the coldest part of the year! Is it traditional for boarding schools to be cold, or are we just lucky? One of the memorable features of being in house is the inescapable cold. Perhaps they think it is character building (or they reckon it will free up the showers faster). After all the learning has been forgotten, part of the education left to each pupil is how to keep warm throughout the year. There is power in the knowledge that late spring can be as cold as early winter, otherwise, it is prone to catch you out and make life a misery.

Personally, I have mastered the fine art of jumper piling. It is essential for existence to know which order hoodies, jumpers and fleece go in order to retain the most heat and to know how many you can pile on whilst still being able to fit through the door (duvet excluded). Just to illustrate the depth of cold experienced and for the sake of history, I am going to relay our true story...

When it became too much for the hoodies, fleeces, sleeping bags and duvets, we decided that we should take a stand, (politican-style rousing speech coming up here.) No longer were we going to accept the necessity of Bunsen burners in the science labs to keep warm. No longer were we going to be cocooned in duvets whilst we watched television. It was time for action. It was time for the Cold Campaign.

At eleven in the evening, we held a dorm meeting (duvets in tow). We chose the centre of the dorm because a broken window at the end of the room was letting in icy drafts, hence, making it a consistent temperature inside and outside of the house. As we huddled together, the whispered discussion bubbled up like steam from a kettle. The outcome was the design for The Cold Campaign.

Everybody in the dorm set to work doing the stuff that they were best at; the more articulate ones decided to write some signs whilst the arty people created a frosty feeling by drawing icicles and glittery snowflakes. Stalactites were suspended from the ceiling and icicles framed the pin boards. White paper was rolled up to form snow on the ground and a cut-out snowman with a huge scarf on was frosted to the window. The poor snowman had frost bite on his fingers and he was trying to claw his way out of the window to a more comfortable zero temperature. There was no danger of this one melting!

If the pictures did not convey the message, then the words certainly did. A death certificate was drawn up for all of the people in the dorm with the cause of death being hypothermia and a pleading request to the cleaners to please leave the curtains to retain what little heat remained in the dorm. The messages were appropriately backed onto blue paper and hung from the lights with long pieces of cotton.

This posed a bit of a problem, as nobody was above 5'6". To overcome this slight setback, I skilfully scaled onto the cubi walls and jumped onto the packti in order to lean over as far as possible whilst someone held onto me. This in itself was a precarious stunt but combined with the fact that it was two hours after lights out so all operations were carried out in the dark, *it was silly*.

Unfortunately, in mid acrobatics, the house mistress chose to walk into the dorm. Oops. Hmmm…how to explain this one? Passing it off as a loo trip was probably not going to work. We were in trouble. Nobody moved. Luckily, the house mistress didn't bother to put the lights on so we were instructed to get back to bed without removing anything.

Nobody could possibly mistake how desperate we were to prove our point—not even standing on scissors and pins could deter us. Have you ever tried to find sellotape in the dark? If you have, you can appreciate why we kept losing ours.

In the morning our protest basked in its own glory for all to see. In the afternoon, after being the talk of the house and our exhibition had been viewed by many members of staff, the verdict was delivered in the temperature of the radiators which were, dum-dum-da…verging on tepid. Progress! Meanwhile, back in the dorms, a strange reaction to blankets was still being observed.

Did I mention the showers? Well, if you are lucky enough to find a shower that locks because of the minimal amount of rust, then you have to contend with the icy dribble that trickles out of the shower head. It takes at least a week after each holiday to have any form of hot water. The whole house shares the two showers that actually have plastic doors and not plastic, grimy curtains that stick to you and chase you around the shower along with the spiders. Sometimes you share your shower with a flying daddy long legs who was looking for a home (the nest is probably in the tiles which bend out from the wall).

To overcome these inconveniences, it is advisable to set an alarm clock at an unsociable hour. No longer will you have to stand in a queue. No longer will you have to stand in other people's dead skin cells. No longer will you have to wipe the bubbles of grime left on the wall by the previous occupant. All you will have to do is expect abuse from the dorm for waking them up early.

May I advise you that if you are still thinking of sending your child to boarding school, consider visiting at an unusual time, during term time, and avoid open day. This will enable you to ponder if you study (and live) comfortably if you took off your coat and scarf and hat. No, not the gloves, leave those on, that would be asking just too much!

Social Life

It's the lunch time on the day of the social! Apples have been gourmandised and the delights of no-frills teabags have been left to stew. Excitement abounds for the evening disco and those who are lucky enough to participate have only the afternoon to get ready. Panic buttons everywhere! There is only enough time to work through each and every item of clothing before systematically discarding it all.

By 7:30 p.m. the dorm is buried under discarded clothes strewn all over the floor after they have been tried and rejected with the scream, "It makes me look fat and it doesn't match." Or, "It's last month's fashion, it looks sooo old," or, "Does this look too slutty?" The next thing to consider is, "Can you see my bra through this dress? Does anyone have a strapless bra I can borrow, please?" The urgent plea echoes through the dorm and there is always someone who tries to resolve the issue.

After the hard decision of what to wear has been sorted, the frantic actions continue with the quest for matching shoes and make-up. The eye shadow matches the dress in this week's fashion and glitter highlights the hair to reflect the disco lights. Eye lashes have been curled with something that resembles an instrument of torture. The finishing touches come in the form of heels. Yes, heels. The bane of my life.

At this point, people realise that it is impossible to squash your feet into high heels and have the bonus luxury of the apparently distant concept of comfort. This is the time to practise teetering around in heels so that you can make that ever-so-important entrance without falling flat on your face. After all, the attractivity of a broken ankle probably would not be recognised amongst the fashion pages of *Vogue*. It is also the time when you start to curse under your breath for picking such a tall pair of heels that the high points of Mount Everest would be hard pressed to compete with them, and yet you are forced to keep smiling whilst enduring chronic spadefuls of pain.

For the next hour, the price, colour and effect of lipstick, nail polishes and foundation are discussed and any recommendations are passed on. Everything seems to be going ok when a glance in the mirror and there facing you is a huge mountain topped by an unsightly yellow mass. Agggghhhhhh! In any make-up manual, this is an example of a most unfortunate curse: a SPOT! It must have grown up during the day (how inconsiderate of it).

The victim wails, "Why did it have to be today? Why didn't somebody say something?" The truth is that it had been quietly observed instead of one stating the obvious, "Well, if nothing can be done, there is no point in causing distress." The offending disfigurement is hastily squeezed but disappointingly to no noticeable effect (only a red rash around the spot, but nobody mentions that).

As a last resort, out comes the "tool box." Quickly, spot cream, concealer and at least one inch of foundation are applied until the spot is completely buried, but the person still insists they can see it.

At last, it is nearly time to move out of the suffocating room of oversprayed perfumes and deodorants. The last layer of lipstick is plastered on and the final glance in the mirror is taken before everyone is ready to leave. Together we face the disco, but the dangerous part is in walking down the seemingly massive amount of steps (wearing heels definitely distorts judgement of this sort of thing) from the boarding house to the Great Hall.

Have you wondered why girls walk down the steps in groups? It is because if, especially as an early teenager, they are not used to short, tight skirts and heels, they have to waddle for mutual support and balance. It is essential to hold onto each other, the support is both physical and mental.

As we enter the disco hall, the pungent smell of over-splashed aftershave vibrates in your nostrils with a rather nauseating effect. That is why it is important to enter the room slowly so that the rank smell is not too overpowering. On first inspection, the boys look as though they have no notion of hygiene and have thrown a bottle of aftershave over themselves in an attempt to hide it. Mostly, they look like they have rolled out of bed and slipped on a t-shirt and jeans.

The party scene is now set in a format that is familiar to most people at some stage in their lives; the girls dance in one sector of the hall, and far, far away from the divide down the centre of the hall is where everything remotely male adheres together and approach the crossing of the invisible divide as though they were about to be hung by the scrotum until infertile. This continues for the first forty minutes as everyone dances awkwardly whilst watching everybody else.

When the time is ripe, there is eager whispering and eventually a boy gets dragged to the divide absolutely mortified whilst his friend asks a girl if she would dance with him. The first couple to dance triggers off a flood of couples making the spectre of someone approaching your group inevitable. When they do, it is always one person who has been nominated as a spokesperson for the group whilst everybody else hangs back eagerly awaiting a response.

It normally goes something like this: it is pitch black, with the exception of the flashing disco lights, and the music is so loud that you have to lip read anyway. Initially, the boy has to make sure that he is speaking to the right girl so there is desperate lip reading of, "This one?" and wild pointing going on between him and his friends. The boy says, "Will you go with my mate?" The natural question (if you understood what they said) is, "Who are you talking about?" They then vaguely indicate that the boy in question is part of a moving mass in the darkness and expect you to make a decision based on that. Apparently, it is meant to be appealing.

At this stage, the girl needs to discuss the answer with her friends; "So what do you reckon?" It has been known for someone to accept the offer but when they see them in the light, they have deeply regretted it. They recount the disgusting mixture of saliva and exchange of tongues. Urgh, why does it have to be so sloppy? Occasionally, if they were very unlucky, the boy had a streaming cold and was using the darkness to his advantage. I shall describe no more.

There appears to be no reasoning behind this method of delegating the task to a friend of asking someone, who you don't even know the name of, for a snog. Perhaps it is in case the girls think that you are a bit forward but it is a forward question afterall. Sometimes, upon seeing the boys approach your group, there is a subtle signal which means to go to the loos and discuss the action plan whilst the boys try their luck elsewhere. It is normal for the boys to bet on who can pull the most girls in one evening. To continue adding to the insult, they have the cheek to call *us* the slags.

It sometimes happens that you are left alone, leaving you free to scan the darkness to see what is on offer. Any bargains left? After a few minutes of disappointment, the fittest guy on the planet can be spotted dancing in the middle of the room with some of his friends. He is so phwoar that he makes your knees buckle. Your luck is in. This is the time to keep cool.

After a quick deliberation, the decision to ask him to dance is made and you make your way across the room to introduce yourself. Violins please! Ah, if music be the food of love, play on. You pull aside people in your way and become immune to the embarrassment of walking into hugging couples. There is now only one person between you—don't back out now. You're nearly there. The last person is pulled out of the way and wow, there in front of you…is his stunning girlfriend. The smile is now reduced to being held up with two fingers as you acknowledge them politely, but what you say doesn't matter because it is not possible to hear them anyway.

Time to root out friends again as the party winds down. When the night is over and the guests have gone, we are left to clear up all the decorations that have been pulled down, popped balloons and any other rubbish that remains. Eventually it is the early hours of the morning when we reach the dorm.

There is a synchronised removal of shoes and resting of blistered feet on the chairs. The steam rises and there is a different aroma mixing with stale perfume. Now is the time for gossip. Every single movement of the male species is recounted and certain unpleasant people are named and shamed to be avoided in the future. The snippets of reportable conversation go like this:

"Did you see the one with the striped shirt who tried to chat up everybody? Nobody would bother with him with that greasy hair and acne."

"Spill the goss. What happened with that freak you were with?"

"Oh, he is soooo gorgeous, I think I'm in love!"

"Do you want a remedy for a hickey?"

The exchange of gossip continues into the morning until the excitement fades and sleep falls to close the eyelashes. This marks the end in one sense but it is only really the beginning, because the following week is the elaboration and clarification of any scandalous issues that happened at the social.

The sixth form balls are a rather grand affair, but however much it might try to be denied, it is a mature version of a social. A large difference is that it is a fabulous excuse to dress up in ball gowns and the boys, some of whom might actually be friends by now, have toned down or indeed changed their aftershave and now dress in black ties, thus making them highly acceptable!

It is a custom that just before the ball begins, all of the sixth formers go around the junior boarding houses to parade their attire in front of the admiring younger years so that everybody can share in the biannual glamour and leave them with the aspiration that, one day, they too will be able to join in the raucous event that creates and destroys many teen relationships. How fun!

Summer Term

Summer Events

Strawberry Tea

This is a quaint tradition that occurs in the middle of the summer term. There is a tennis tournament for parents and their children to participate in on the school grounds. The name of the event is due to the afternoon tea that is provided after the tennis because all of the food has strawberries in it. The food is a buffet-style meal in the dining hall and has piles of strawberries and cream for people to eat.

Inter-House Fashion Show

The sixth formers in each house are responsible for organising the show right from the topic chosen through to overseeing the costumes and choreography. The whole house is split into groups of people who are either going to model or those who want to work back stage. The next few weeks are made up of madly making costumes from simple materials like bin bags, cotton and paints. When the costumes are finished, they show real, skill as bin bags are transformed into dresses painted with spiders. One house has been known to make all of their costumes out of crisp packets and bits of rubbish.

Extra stage blocks to form a catwalk are placed at the end of the stage in the Great Hall. There is a strict timetable about when each house can use the hall to practise to ensure that time is fairly allocated. Parents and people from the local village are invited to watch the fashion show. The houses are judged on their costume and choreography by people selected from the surrounding design colleges.

Sports Day

Quite a major day! This is a showcase for all of the athletic people in the school. As usual, the houses are set against each other and everyone has to participate in at least one event. There are several events on the running track, javelin, discus, long jump etc. that take place throughout the day so that people can score points for their house. The parents arrive in their four-wheel drives completely prepared to be comfortable for the whole day. It is quite a feat of packing but a whole set of chairs, tables and parasols are stored in the boot of the car. In order to complete the show, there are the large crystal bowls of strawberries and the flask is put aside in favour of champagne.

A large marquee has been pitched up by the side of the running track for the occasion. Inside the marquee are several tables of the usual food such as sandwiches and cakes for everyone. The kitchen staff are dressed in their uniform and oversee that everything inside the marquee runs smoothly.

Late afternoon heralds the end of the events. All pupils sit on the grass in front of the pavillion in the centre of the sports field. Certificates are awarded to those who have broken school records, accompanied by applause. The house with the most points is given a cup as a prize—loud cheering for this one! For those people who have room for more food then an afternoon tea is provided in the dining hall.

Leavers' Weekend

This weekend is of the utmost importance to the school, not to mention the sixth formers, because this is their two-day goodbye ceremony. On the last Saturday of term, it is the Walkdown service on the quad, followed by a formal prize-giving ceremony in the Great Hall where the dignitaries sit on the stage. The day afterwards is the morning Leaving Service in the Church that follows the format of hymns, sermon and the traditional Rutter's "Gaelic Blessing" to finish everything off. But, it carries far too much importance for me to let you know about it yet, oh yes, there are hours and hours of rehearsals ahead of us first!

The first practice sees the entire school assembled inside the Great Hall in their Forms. The purpose of this is to get everybody in height order from the most petite to the tallest, hence the name of the task is "heighting." The process is helped by the fact that people try to sort themselves out before the teacher walks around to them. It takes an absolute age.

When this is sorted, people are then grouped into which boarding house they will be standing behind for the walkdown. Morning assembly is replaced by the forty-minute practice five days a week for the unaccompanied hymns on the amphitheatre and the slow, syncronised walkdown. This is time when the music teachers try their hardest to force everyone to learn the dry school prayer, "I lift mine eyes up to hills…" and the school hymn, "Heavenly Father Who Has Taught Us." Mr. Jones threatens that when we all leave school and get married, we will go all sentimental and want this at our weddings. Hmmm…

Mini-Speech Day
This is the little baby speech day when only the pupils and staff are present. It is the time for all of those drama, music and sports prizes to be given out. The prize recipients have all practised the correct timing and format for going onto the stage: walk up to the top of the stairs when the last person has walked off the other end of the stage, shake with the right hand, take with the left, turn to the right and smile. The audience dutifully applaud everyone so its all very cricket.

Morning of Speech Day
This tradition cannot be forgotten because it is really good fun. All of the boarders hold hands to form a circle in the quad after breakfast. We then all sing "Auld Lang Zine" whilst running forwards and back again in one big mass of people. Great opportunity to make a lot of noise and stand on the sacred grass on the quad.

Speech Day

Walkdown

Drum roll please! This is *the main* event in the school's calendar. For the pupils, it is an endless nightmare. It is the climax of weeks of rehearsing hymns and repeatedly walking up and down the amphitheatre in preparation for a twenty-minute service that was devised to celebrate the opening of the boarding houses, but in the event of rain, it might not even take place.

Now, no service would run smoothly without the monumental effort from the music department. Our favourite Mr. Coward progressively works himself into a visible sweat in anticipation of the singing to come. During hymn practices, a week before the grand occasion, he stands on his box in front of the whole school and begins to conduct vigorously. It may be early on a cool morning, but he waves his arms about with such energy in a futile attempt to drag sound out of the school that he has to wipe the dripping sweat off his brow. He bounces up and down on his box until everyone is certain that it will snap from under him or throw him off like a spring board. I hear that this is the main focus for the parents' attention during the church service.

This is only the beginning. Ten minutes into the practice he slowly strips off his jumper and loosens his tie like a proper Chippendale (phwoar, we wish he was!) Steady girls! He lifts his arms high into the air in an attempt to pitch a high note when he invariably creates his own key and all he succeeds in doing is to reveal huge sweat patches under his arms (our real hope of pitching the right note is to sit next to the piano).

He loses so much weight through sweating that he frequently has to pause the rehearsal to pull up his trousers which have started to slip down and he also has to tuck in his shirt which has begun to fly around. As the stress mounts, his chest expands and his buttons are in danger of popping off.

One day when a pupil politely pointed out that he was showing just too much chest for that time in the morning, he sent her to Head's office with the explicit instruction that she had to explain why she had been sent there. All of his enthusiasm is finally shown when he rubs himself like a cricketer just before he is about to bowl in a vital match but he doesn't have a…awww! I should not say that! Sometimes he gets so excited that it looks like he will rub a big hole in his trousers. By this stage, it is the end of the practice, which is quite fortunate because everyone is in stitches, but Mr Coward does not know why.

At 11:00, it is time for "Walkdown" to begin. The pupils are lined up in height order—smallest first (thanks to heighting which occurs several weeks before hand; the whole school has to be put into height order in the Great Hall) and are hidden behind the three boarding houses at the top of the amphitheatre. The parents are on the grassy quad at the bottom of the amphitheatre. Everyone waits in silent anticipation; Mr Coward sweats.

The large bell is rung three times. Hopefully, especially if you are leading out from the side, you hear the third bell because that is the signal to start counting: one elephant, two elephant, three elephant…until seven elephant and that is the point to start walking so that all four lines of pupils meet in the same place at the same time. The people behind the central boarding house (Andies—yay!) start to walk immediately after the third bell. This is a very intricate stepping movement and once you get the rhythm in motion, if anyone fell out of step, it would have a disasterous domino effect. We have not practised that.

If all goes according to plan, the four lines meet, two from the front boarding houses and two from Andies. As you can appreciate, there is plenty of room for error, so we have to practice and practice. Dominoes are not accepted. All it needs is for one person to lose their footing on a chipped step to start a cascade of people down the amphitheatre. Oops!

The service includes the school prayer, which despite the hardest effort of the teachers, nobody can remember. The prayer is mostly mumbled (large percentage of the noise coming from the choir who have the words in their music folder) and the loudest part is "Amen." The support plan is to mime the alphabet to give the appearance of speaking the prayer but everyone mimes different letters at the same time so it is undecided if the plan works. Some people take a small copy of the words in their blazer pockets and discretely slip it under the collar of the person's blazer in front of them during the service.

As people perch on the amphitheatre in rows, the sun begins to show its full July strength. The dress code, let me remind you, is Formal Uniform: long, grey woollen socks pulled up to the knee, met by a black, two-inch-below-the-knee, straight, itchy skirt, burgundy and white-striped blouse complete with ribbon tie, black jumper and to finish, the burgundy blazer. Why does this school always force us to dress in layers?

Not surprisingly, it gets very hot and people feel as though they are emulating Mr. Coward. It has been known for the heat to reach too much of a high point so that somebody fainted. Crisis! Keep smiling! Do not worry, we have practised for just such an occasion. The two people next to her follow the procedure which is to slowly close up the gap, leaving the person to sit on the amphitheatre out of sight behind them whilst the school nurse sees to her. There, the image of the school is saved.

After Walkdown, there is a long speech and prize-giving service in the Great Hall. This is the worst part of the day because most of the school has to squash onto wooden tiers which make your bum ache (the parents get comfy seats, whatever happened to equal rights?). After the first twenty minutes, it becomes imperative to move a little but nobody dares. The only option is to discretely shift from one side of your arse to the other for a very long two hours—oh the pain! You simply have to have your hands together on your lap, back straight, legs straight, with the ankles loosely crossed with yet another glued smile whilst not forgetting to clap after every single person has received their prize.

Another element of tradition is displayed by the five flower girls. This is a privileged position because only first years with the best textbook posture (training involves walking around with a hymn book placed on their head) are chosen to curtsey to the main guests (school governors and guest speakers) who are on the main stage throughout the main service and are presented with a bunch of flowers for their efforts. It is rather sexist, but the male guests are left with nothing.

The following day (Sunday) the end of the school year is heralded with a Leavers' Service and afternoon tea in the dining hall. In normal Sunday services, the uniform includes a cloak to look smart (and keep warm—no parents, no heating). No walkmans today though!

At one particular service, the archbishop was delivering the sermon and entered with the usual pomp and ceremony of the choir being his entourage.

He talked quite fluently (in his heavy Welsh accent) for a few minutes but suddenly stopped mid-word and his mouth stuck in the shape of a yawn. It remained frozen in this state for ten minutes. Initially, people tried to ignore the fact that the archbishop had forgotten his words and was in a state of otherworldliness.

He paused for so long that the whispering began and people contemplated calling for an ambulance, convinced that he had suffered a heart attack. Suddenly, he began talking again from where he left off. It was, how shall I put this, an *interesting* use of the suspensory pause. The service always ends with Rutter's "A Gaelic Blessing" as a final goodbye to the sixth formers.

At the end of the service, the sixth formers are customarily red-eyed because they are leaving their friends and the school they have known for at least seven years for the last time (although friends always keep in touch, these people are friends for life). Thirty minutes later they are fine and have forgotten all about it. Their leaving makes way for the next intake of first years so that they too can enjoy the memories and instilled attitudes that have been recounted in this book. Personally, I would not have missed it for the world, and although am no longer in daily attendance at school, its character-forming influence is still with me.

Printed in the United Kingdom
by Lightning Source UK Ltd.
114207UKS00001BA/33